*For Gavin and Liam, and
chasing your dreams. - D.S*

*I dedicate this book to my favorite teacher
Ms. Teri Carter. I'm an author because of you! - I.B*

devin@devincomedy.com

Website: www.devincomedy.com

 facebook.com/devinsieboldcomedy

 @devinsiebold

 @devinsiebold

 youtube.com/devinsiebold

A TEACHER IN THE ZOO

Devin Siebold

Illustrated by Izzy B

IzzyBBooks

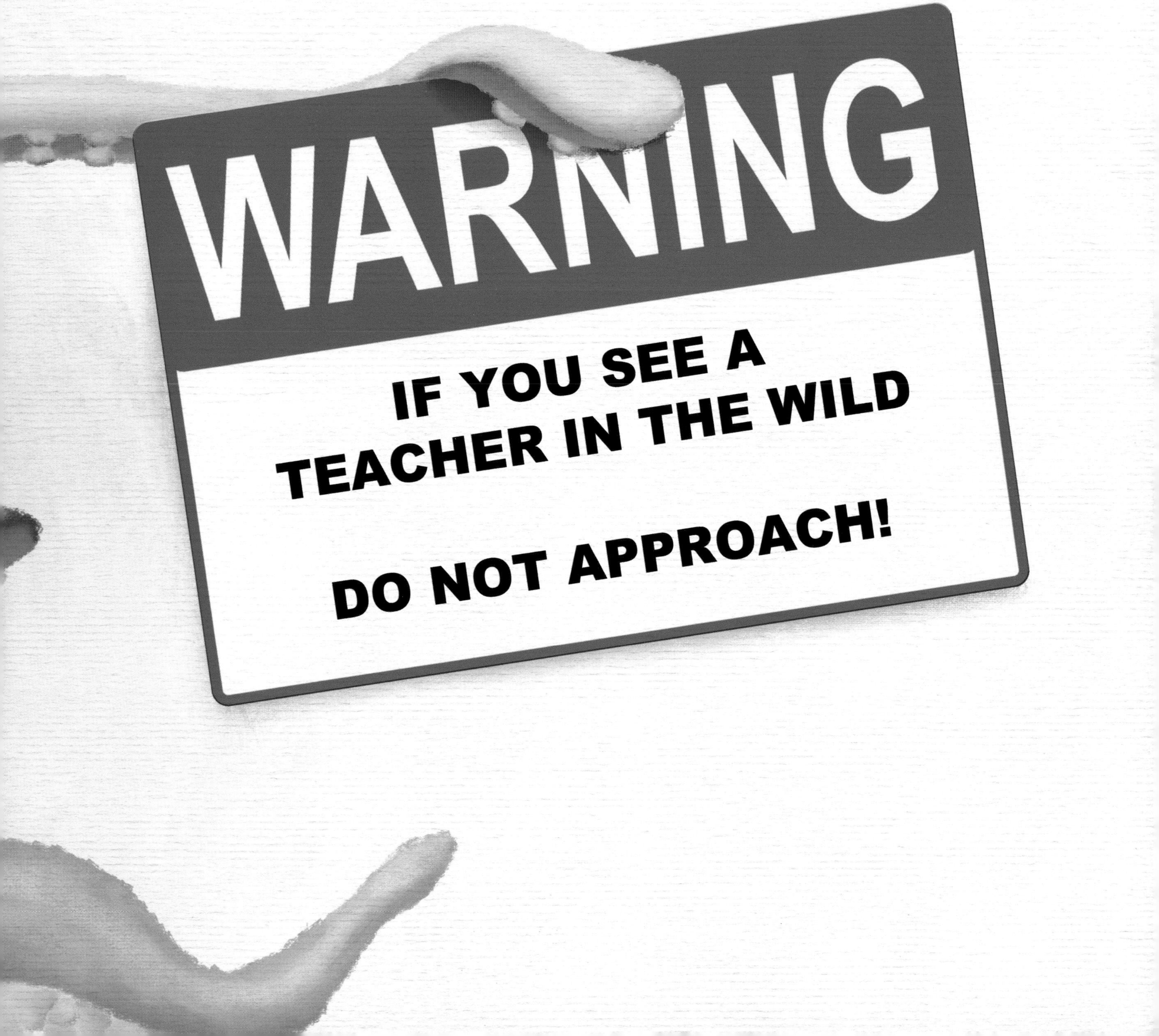
WARNING
IF YOU SEE A
TEACHER IN THE WILD
DO NOT APPROACH!

Was it a joyous mall trip
for the new game now on sale?
Or a nightmare in disguise?
Heed caution in my tale.

For this is a story of terror
of a father and a child
who narrowly escaped
a teacher in the wild.

The drive was pretty normal.
Then we entered inside the lot.
I saw a car like Mrs. Brown's.
"It COULDN'T be", I thought.

She never leaves the school.
Why on earth would she be out?
Unless that WASN'T Mrs. Brown!
I had better sneak and scout.

The first clue that it wasn't her
was the t-shirt and some jeans.
I see her each and every day.
She'd never worn those things!

Then there was her smiling face.
It looked so carefree.
Not nearly as stressed out
as she was in class with me.

Oh look, it seems she's shopping.
She's checking out the shoes.
That looks innocent enough,
but it could just be a ruse.

Maybe she's an alien,
and her ship is landing soon.
And she needs a special pair of shoes
to abduct kids to the moon.

Then onto the jewelery store,
where she's checking out a charm.
Quite normal, you may feel and think,
but I say sound the alarm!

For everybody surely knows
that teachers are always broke.
Could this be a magical wizard
in need of crystals for her cloak!?

Her last stop is in the book store,
but if she wanted to read,
well, school had an entire library
of all she would ever need.

Therefore, she must be a witch!
She's shopping for her spells,
so she can turn us all to chickens
at the sound of a classroom bell.

I've got to warn my schoolmates
of this teacher-stealing stranger.
If she makes it back to school
we're all in serious danger.

I said, "Dad we have to go!"
But he ignored my warning call,
and I saw him wave at someone
that was just across the mall.

Oh no! It can't be true.
Mrs. Brown was on her way!
Run while you still can,
or we'll both become her prey.

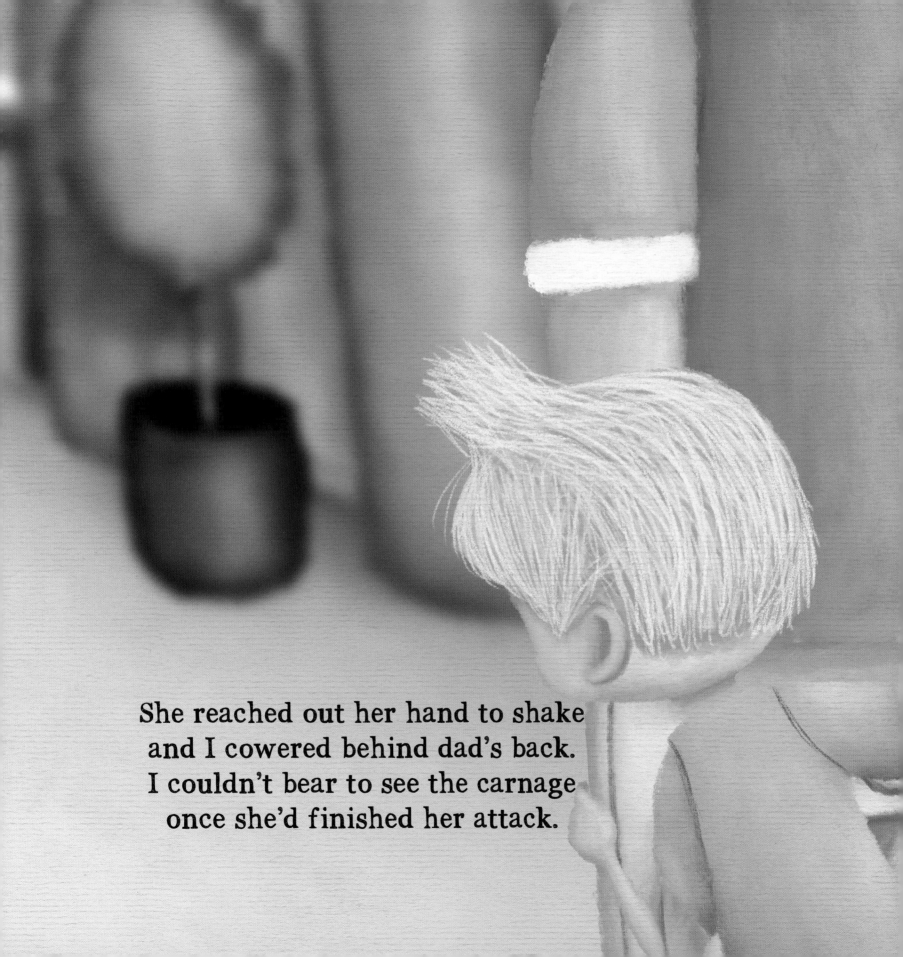

She reached out her hand to shake
and I cowered behind dad's back.
I couldn't bear to see the carnage
once she'd finished her attack.

Did her tentacles wrap around him?
Is she brain washing his mind?
Maybe melting his face to goo?
Or ALL those things combined?!

Just then I heard a laugh
and a warm hand on my own.
The subtle kindness in her voice.
A soft, comforting tone.

My eyes opened to Mrs. Brown
and all her wonderful features.
There is no mistaking it now.
This was, indeed, my teacher.

Turns out she is normal
and sometimes leaves the school.
Good thing I wasn't scared,
but my dad sure lost his cool.

"Now let's go buy that game I want,"
but my father seemed delayed.
"Now wait one minute, kiddo,
I want to discuss your grade."

Devin Siebold has always enjoyed a passion for all things creative from the moment he was asked by his third grade teacher to memorize a Shel Silverstein poem. From that point on he knew he wanted to be a writer. In grade school he won several writing competitions and filled endless notebooks with children's poetry, stories, and curiosities. Throughout college Devin explored musical outlets and began dabbling in scripts. As a professional teacher, he found sketch writing and stand-up comedy to be a stress reliever, and even discovered a way to turn it into a second career option. Now, as a full-time comedian and content producer, Devin has circled back around to his first love: creative writing and poetry for children. Publishing "A Teacher in the Wild" is a dream come true, but the journey doesn't end there. Still writing, still curious, and forever entrenched in an over-active imagination, expect much, much more in the future from Devin Siebold.

Izzy B is the author of A Tighty-Whitie Wind and other super silly books. He dreamed of being an author illustrator since the first grade. As a kid he often spent his time creating funny stories and drawing quirky pictures. When Izzy grew up he became an elementary school teacher and fell in love with books. During his time as a teacher Izzy loved sharing his stories with his students. That passion grew and grew. Now he makes books full time and illustrates stories for other authors. Izzy now hopes to inspire young authors to love reading and writing like he did.

www.izzybbooks.com